HeNRY HECKELBECK

and the Not-So-Dark Day

By **Wanda Coven**

Illustrated by **Priscilla Burris**

LITTLE SIMON
New York Amsterdam/Antwerp London Toronto
Sydney/Melbourne New Delhi

This book is a work of fiction. Any references to historical events, real people, or real places are used fictitiously. Other names, characters, places, and events are products of the author's imagination, and any resemblance to actual events or places or persons, living or dead, is entirely coincidental.

LITTLE SIMON
An imprint of Simon & Schuster Children's Publishing Division
1230 Avenue of the Americas, New York, New York 10020
First Little Simon hardcover edition June 2025
© 2025 by Simon & Schuster, LLC
Also available in a Little Simon paperback edition.

For information about special discounts for bulk purchases, please contact Simon & Schuster Special Sales at 1-866-506-1949 or business@simonandschuster.com. The Simon & Schuster Speakers Bureau can bring authors to your live event. For more information or to book an event contact the Simon & Schuster Speakers Bureau at 1-866-248-3049 or visit our website at www.simonspeakers.com.
Designed by Chrisila Maida
Manufactured in the United States of America 0525 LAK
10 9 8 7 6 5 4 3 2 1
Library of Congress Cataloging-in-Publication Data
Names: Coven, Wanda, author. | Burris, Priscilla, illustrator.
Title: Henry Heckelbeck and the not-so-dark day / by Wanda Coven ; illustrated by Priscilla Burris. | Description: First Little Simon paperback edition. | New York : Little Simon, 2025. | Series: Henry Heckelbeck ; book 18 | Audience term: Children Summary: A city blackout causes school to be canceled, but Henry has a great time playing flashlight limbo with his friends, making shadow puppets, and even getting to eat all the ice cream before it melts.
Identifiers: LCCN 2024040432 (print) | LCCN 2024040433 (ebook)
ISBN 9781665962964 (paperback) | ISBN 9781665962971 (hardcover)
ISBN 9781665962988 (ebook) | Subjects: CYAC: Electric power failures—Fiction. | Play—Fiction. | Classification: LCC PZ7.C83393 Hbo 2025 (print) | LCC PZ7.C83393 (ebook) | DDC [Fic]—dc23
LC record available at https://lccn.loc.gov/2024040432
LC ebook record available at https://lccn.loc.gov/2024040433

CONTENTS

Chapter 1

SOMETHING DIFFERENT

Henry's spy senses tingled.

Something is different about this morning, he thought as he sat up in bed. *But what?*

Henry looked around his room.

His books stood on the bookshelves. Outside his window, clouds covered the sun in the sky.

Everything looked totally normal.

Already fully dressed, Henry jumped out of bed and flicked on the light switch. But the light didn't turn on.

Flick! Flick! Flick!

Nothing happened.

So Henry ran into the hallway and thumped down the stairs.

"The light fizzed out in my room!" he yelled.

Right outside the kitchen, Henry's spy senses tingled again.

It's too quiet, he thought.

There was no toaster dinging. No smoothie machine whirring. No music playing or Dad humming.

Henry trotted into the kitchen. His mom and dad were sitting at the table in their pajamas.

Pajamas on a Thursday morning? Something was *definitely* weird!

"What's going on?" he asked.
"Is today April Fool's Day?"

"No fooling around," Dad
said. "Brewster is having a
blackout."

Henry gasped.

"A blackout?" Henry said. "Like, all the lights are out?"

"The main power line is down," Mom told Henry. "The electricity is out all over town. Even at school."

Henry asked, "Does that mean I have to go to school in the DARK?"

Mom and Dad laughed.

"No, silly," Dad said. "It means there's no school today."

Henry's face lit up. "No school" were the two most magical words on a Thursday morning! "YES!" he shouted.

His spy senses were right, after all!

Chapter 2

POWER PLAY

Dad handed Henry a shiny pocket flashlight.

"This is your blackout gadget, Henry the Spy," Dad said with a wink.

Henry loved gadgets.

Henry pushed the squishy button on the flashlight.

Click! Click! The light had a high beam and a low beam.

Henry ran upstairs, clicking the flashlight on and off as he went.

His sister, Heidi, was reading in her room by flashlight.

"Tag, you're it!" Henry said, shining a beam of light into the room.

"Hey!" Heidi yelled. "Who said you could barge into my room without knocking?"

She grabbed a pillow and chucked it at Henry.

"Missed me by a mile!"
Henry said. "So, you wanna
play flashlight tag?"

"I'm reading," Heidi replied.
"Play by yourself."

"Come on!" Henry begged.
"You need more than one
person to play flashlight tag."

But Heidi just put her nose back into her book.

"You're no fun," Henry huffed, stomping out of the room.

Then he had an idea. *Heidi may not be fun. But Dudley is!*

Dudley Day was Henry's friend. He lived four doors down the street.

Henry bolted out the front door and raced down the sidewalk. That's when he saw someone else running toward him from the other direction.

"HENRY!" Max Maplethorpe shouted, waving a flashlight.

They caught up to each other
in front of Dudley's house.

"No school!" cheered Max.

"No kidding!" said Henry,
giving her a high five.

Just as they were about to knock, Dudley's front door flung open.

"I've been waiting all morning for someone to play with!" Dudley said. "Come on. Let's go to my room!"

The friends bounded inside. The blackout fun was about to begin!

Chapter 3

LIGHT AND SHADOW

"Let's play flashlight limbo," suggested Dudley.

They shut the shades, making the room even darker. Then Dudley flashed a beam of light across his room.

"You're out if you touch the beam," Dudley explained. "Okay, GO!"

Henry and Max took turns bending backward under the flashlight's beam. Each round got harder as Dudley lowered the flashlight.

"This is a piece of cake!" Max said as she cleared the beam again.

"Oh yeah?" Dudley said, lowering the flashlight even more. "This time, you have to crab-walk!"

Max crab-walked under the beam, but the rim of her hat touched the light.

"*Zzzzzt!*" buzzed Henry. "You're out!"

Now it was his turn to try. He started crab-walking under the beam of light.

Then . . . *splat!* He landed right on his butt, and they all cracked up.

"Your turn, Dudley!" said Henry.

But Dudley wanted to play a new game. He laid his flashlight on his desk so that the beam of light shone on the wall.

"Now let's make shadow puppets!" he said.

Henry and Max laid their flashlights on the desk too.

Max held her hands to the light and put her thumbs together. Then she spread the rest of her fingers to look like wings.

"Flap! Flap! Flap! It's a shadow bird!" she said.

They made shadow bunnies, snails, deer, and a dog, too.

"Woof! Woof! Woof!" barked Dudley, making his shadow dog's mouth open and close.

Henry tried to make a shadow spider, but he couldn't get it to look right.

"It looks more like a blobby monster," he said.

Max held up two fingers to the blobby monster.

"Now it's a blobby alien monster!" she said, wiggling her fingers.

Dudley used his fingers to add wings. "Now it's a blobby alien monster WITH WINGS!"

The friends marveled at their monstrous creation.

"It looks just like a monster in a scary movie," Dudley said.

"Totally," Max agreed.

That's when a sly grin spread across Henry's face.

"You know who would be freaked out by this shadow?" he said. "My SISTER!"

Chapter 4

GOTCHA!

"Um, are you sure we should scare Heidi?" asked Dudley.

Henry rolled his eyes and said, "I do it all the time! With whoopee cushions, rubber snakes, you name it!"

And besides, Henry thought to himself. *This will be payback for the pillow Heidi threw at me earlier.*

Dudley and Max looked at each other.

"Okay, if you say so!" Max said.

Henry led the way out of Dudley's house and into his own. They tiptoed up the stairs.

"I can't believe we're doing this!" Dudley whispered.

Henry nudged him. "*Shush!* Or you'll blow our cover!"

The three friends crept down the hallway. They stopped outside Heidi's closed door.

Henry put a finger to his lips and placed his ear against the door. Something rustled inside.

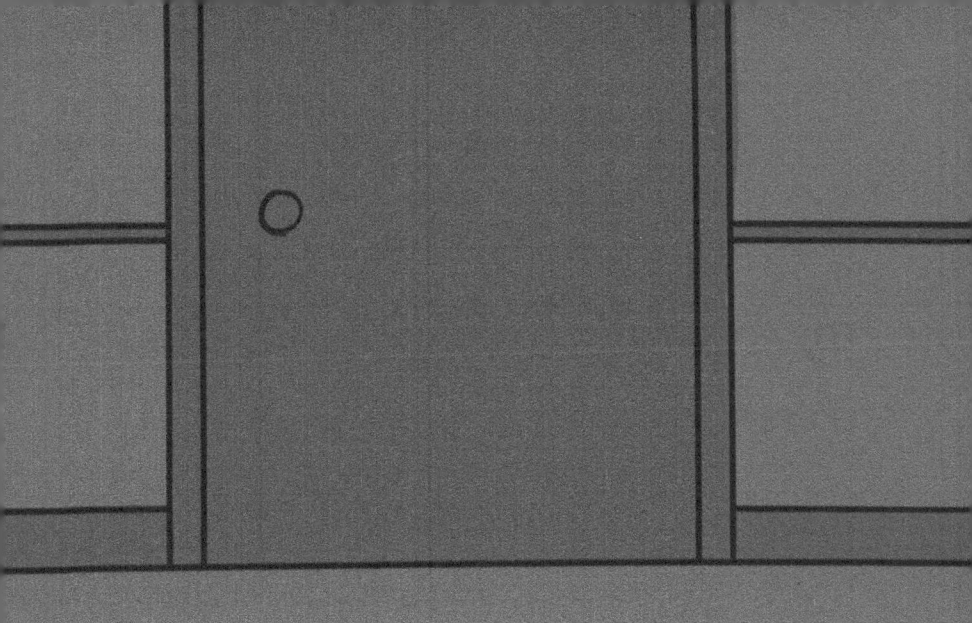

"I hear her in there," he whispered. "Let's make our shadow puppet. Then, on the count of three, I'll open the door and we'll roar like a monster. Okay?"

Dudley clicked on his flashlight and shined it against the wall outside Heidi's room. Then they formed the blobby-alien-shadow-monster.

Henry began to count. "One, two . . ."

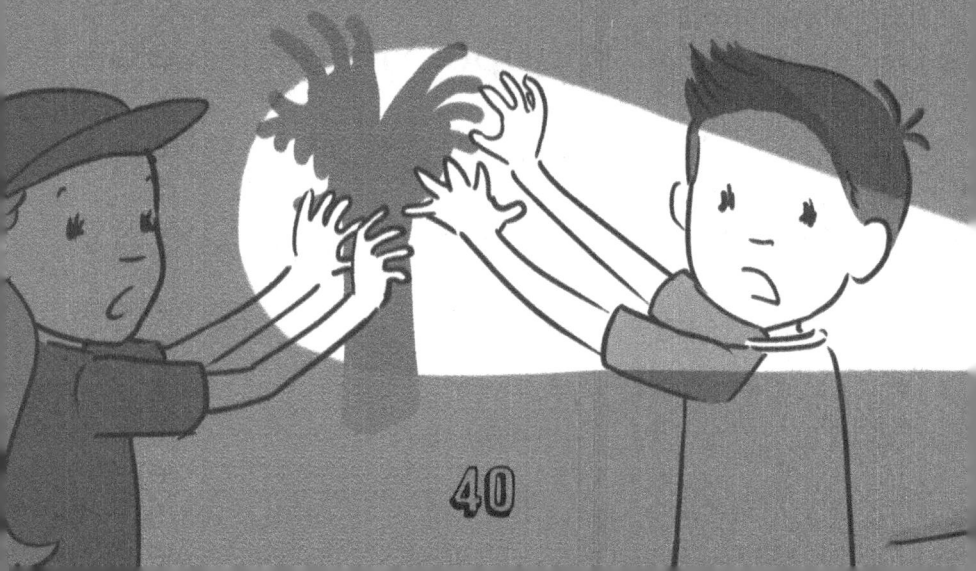

Heidi's door flung open.

"*Roooaaar!*" she shouted.

"AAAAHHH!" yelled Henry, Dudley, and Max.

Heidi had reverse pranked them!

"Nice try," Heidi said, snorting with laughter. "But I could hear you outside my door the whole time!"

"Whoa," Max said. "Your sister is pretty cool, Henry."

But Henry frowned. He did not like being beaten at his own game.

I wanted to be the scary one, Henry thought. *Not the other way around!*

Chapter 5

BLACKOUT COOKOUT

Henry's spy senses tingled again.

"*Mmmm,* I detect the smell of something yummy!" he said, sniffing the air.

"Me too!" Max said.

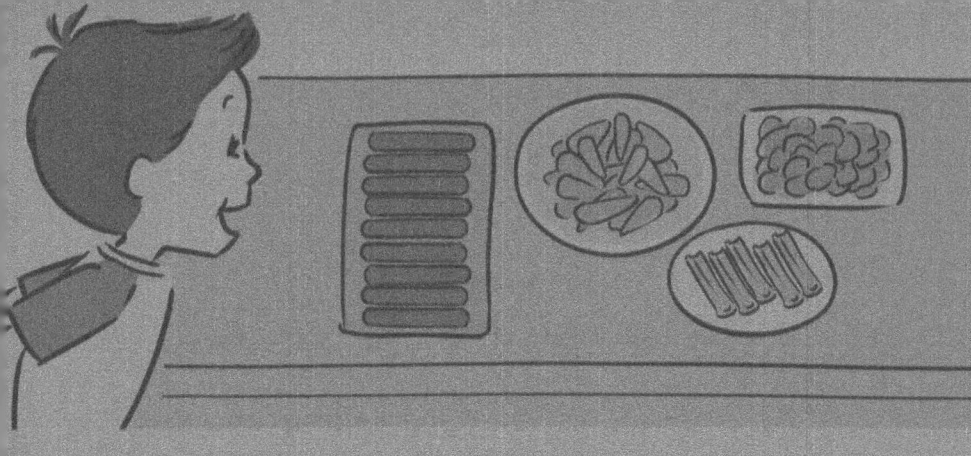

Henry, Dudley, and Max raced downstairs and into the kitchen. The counter was covered with food: hot dogs, carrots, celery, and more!

"This is enough food to feed the whole town!" Henry exclaimed.

Mom was stacking hot dog buns on a tray.

"With the power out, the food in the fridge will spoil," she said. "So, we invited the neighbors for a cookout."

"HOORAY!" Henry, Dudley, and Max shouted.

Outside, Dad was flipping burgers on the grill. The neighbors had brought their own food too, which were placed on foldout tables.

The friends grabbed hot dogs, burgers, carrots, and chips. Then they plunked onto a blanket on the grass to enjoy their blackout feast.

Heidi sat on a different blanket with her best friends, Lucy Lancaster and Bruce Bickerson.

When Henry looked over, Heidi stuck her thumb on her nose and waggled her fingers at him. So Henry did the same back to her.

Max patted her stomach after clearing her plate.

"I'm stuffed," she said.

"Same," agreed Dudley and Henry.

Whap! The screen door slapped open and shut.

"Dessert time!" Mom called.

Henry's face lit up.

"Guess we're not stuffed anymore!" he said.

The dessert table was covered with open ice-cream containers. It was like having a backyard ice-cream shop!

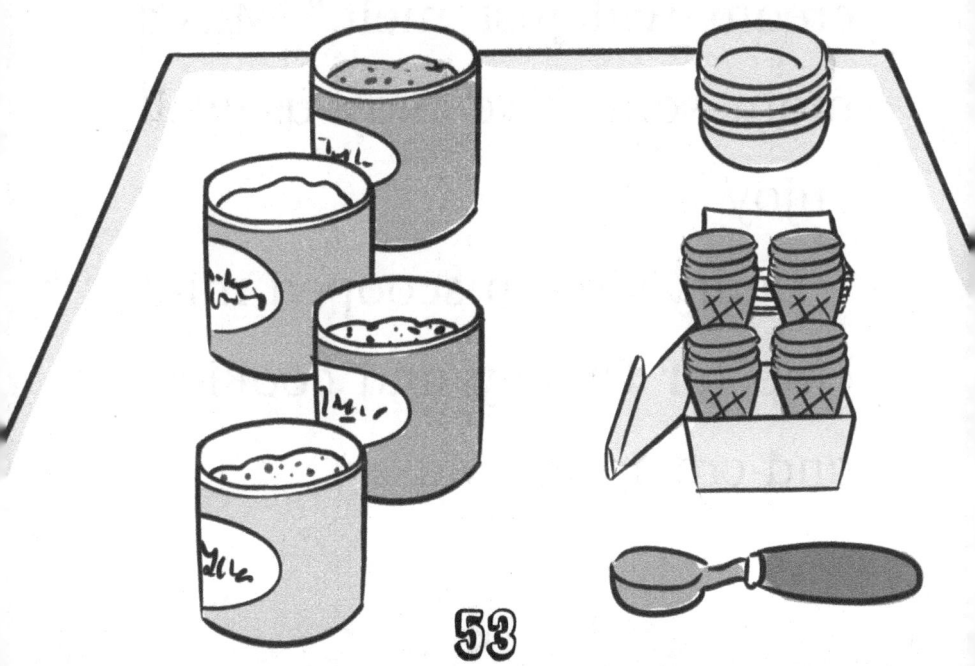

"Without power, the ice cream will just melt," Max's mom said. "We may as well enjoy it!"

Henry's mom scooped mint chip for Dudley and cookies-and-cream for Max.

Henry and Heidi both wanted chocolate chip, but there was only one scoop left.

"I call dibs!" Henry shouted. "Plus, you owe it to me for the reverse prank."

His sister crossed her arms and huffed.

"Fine," Heidi said. "But you have to promise: no more pranks today."

"Deal," Henry replied. "But YOU have to promise no more pranks either."

Heidi held out a pinky finger and asked, "Pinky promise?"

"Pinky promise!" Henry answered, linking his pinky with Heidi's.

Now we're even! Henry thought as he walked away, licking his ice-cream cone.

Chapter 6
HOW TO UNPLUG

After dessert, everyone started packing up to head home, including Dudley and Max.

Henry wasn't ready for the blackout fun to be over, though. He tugged his mom's sweater.

"Can Dudley and Max sleep over tonight?" Henry asked.

The parents looked at each other. It didn't seem like a yes.

"If the power comes on, you'll have school tomorrow," Henry's dad reminded them.

"But we'll go to bed early,"
Henry pleaded. "We promise!"

"We promise! We promise!"
Dudley and Max nodded wildly.

"Okay," Dudley's dad said
slowly. "If the power is still off
at dinnertime, then you may
have a sleepover."

All the parents agreed, so it was decided. Everyone waved goodbye, for now.

Henry marched to his room. He had to make sure the power stayed off until *at least* dinner.

And he knew just the thing to do.

"Magic book, I need you!" he whispered.

The magic book slid off the bookshelf and floated to Henry. He clicked on his flashlight and found the perfect spell.

The Unplugged Spell

Do you wish the power was out? Maybe you want some peace and quiet? Or perhaps you need an excuse for a sleepover? If you're looking to unplug, then this is the spell for you!

Ingredients:
1 flashlight
1 other object that runs on batteries
1 crayon wrapper
1 food item, not from the fridge

gather the ingredients in the darkest spot in your room. Hold your medallion in one hand and shine the flashlight on the pile. Chant the following spell.

Unplug! Unplug!
Turn off the power!
Make it stay off
for over an hour.
Keep it dark into the night.
Then with the dawn,
bring back the light.

Henry peeled the wrapper off a pink crayon. Then he grabbed an old battery-operated toy truck from under his bed. He also snuck some crackers from the pantry.

Henry carried everything into his closet and shut the door.

He held his medallion in one hand and his flashlight in the other. Then he chanted the spell.

Swoosh! Sparkles lit up the closet and quickly faded away.

Henry crawled out of his closet and tested his bedside lamp. It didn't turn on.

He raised his hands in victory.

"Sleepover, here I come!"

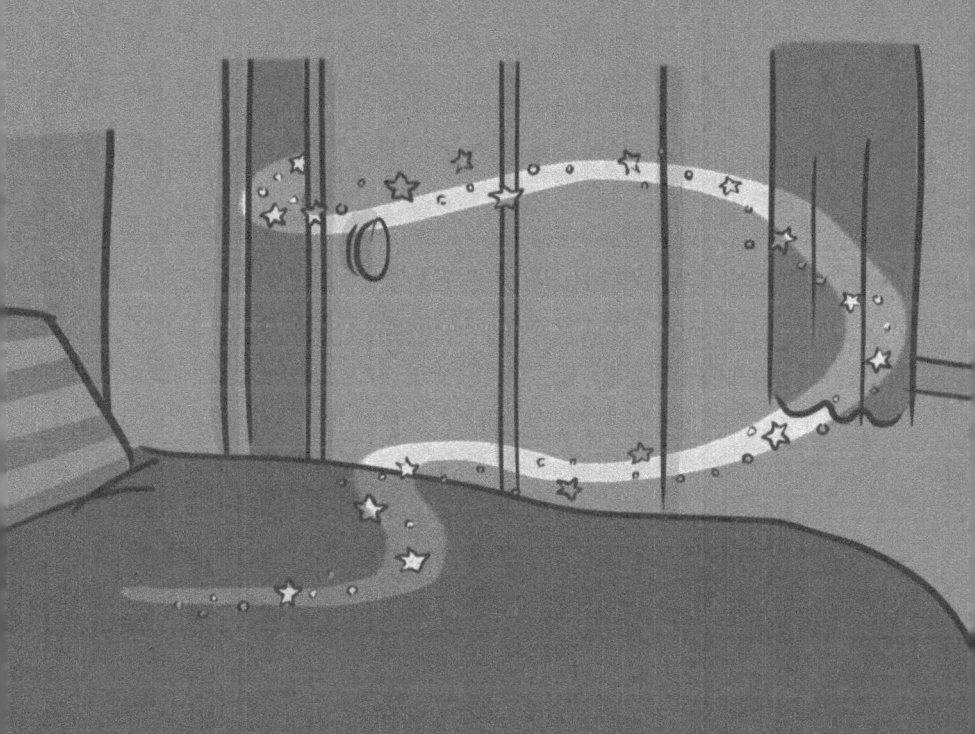

Chapter 7

SLEEPOVER TIME!

The lights were still off at dinnertime.

The spell worked! thought Henry. *Magic is the BEST!*

Max and Dudley came over a while later.

The sun had set outside. It was way too dark to see anything without a flashlight.

The three of them laid out their sleeping bags on the living room carpet.

"Let's play flashlight hide-and-seek," suggested Henry. "I'm IT!"

He slowly counted to twenty-five, while Max and Dudley went to hide.

"Ready or not, here I come!" called Henry.

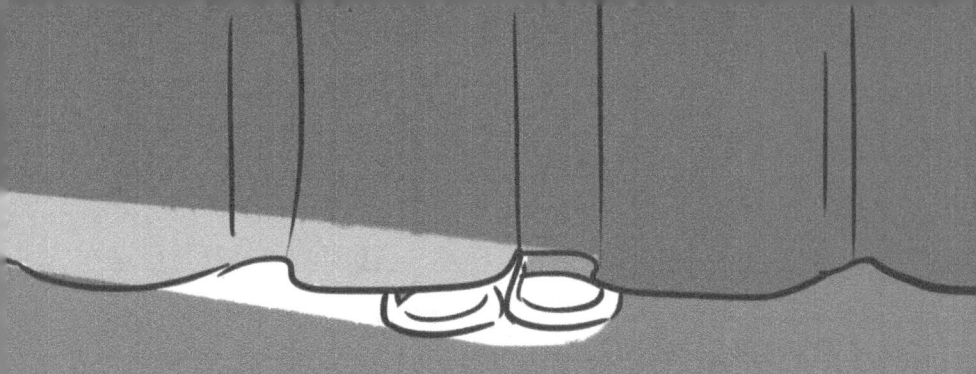

He shined his flashlight
around the room and spied
two feet sticking out from
under a curtain.

Henry crept over and pulled
back the curtain.

"You found me!" Dudley
laughed, shielding his eyes
from the light.

Henry went right back to work. He waved his flashlight around the room again.

Maybe Max is hiding behind the couch, he thought. He tiptoed across the sleeping bags.

"OW!" cried a muffled voice.
Henry shined his beam on a
squirming sleeping bag. Max's
head popped out of it.

"Hey, you stepped on me!"
she said.

"Sorry, I didn't mean to," Henry said. "But I still found you!"

He laid his flashlight on the coffee table. His shadow stretched up to the ceiling.

"Beware of the shadow monster!" Henry roared. "No one can hide from him!"

Max and Dudley wanted in on the fun too.

Three shadow monsters danced in the light, making up silly dance moves.

After a while they collapsed in a heap on top of their sleeping bags.

"Blackouts are the BEST!" said Dudley.

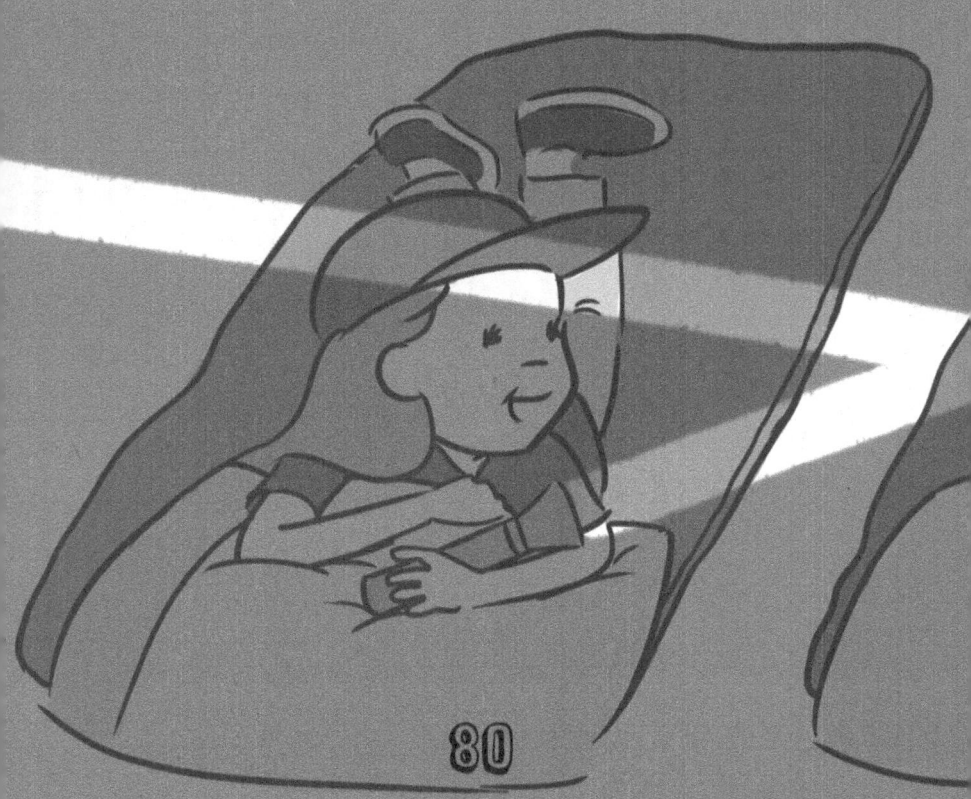

Henry and Max agreed.

Who needed the power on when you could have flashlight sleepovers with your friends?

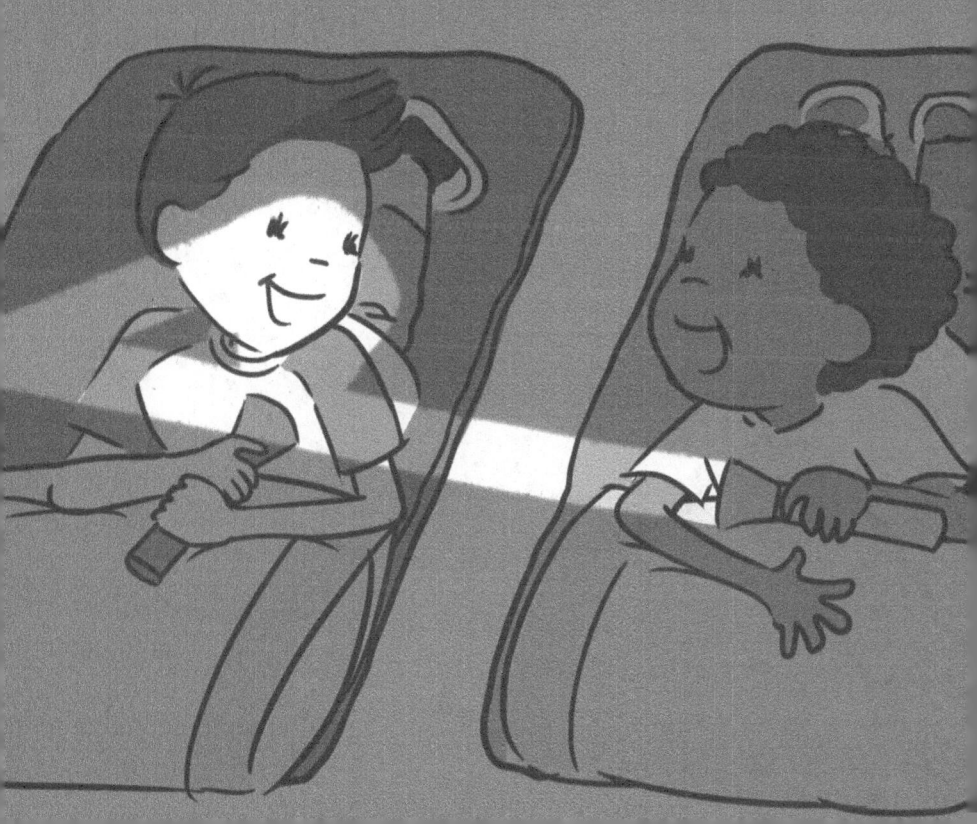

Chapter 8

LIGHTS OUT

"All that dancing made me thirsty!" Dudley said.

Henry, Max, and Dudley pointed their flashlights and headed toward the dark kitchen.

Once they entered, Henry pulled out three glasses from the cupboard.

"Strawberry milk, please!" Henry said to his mom.

But she shook her head.

"Sorry, Henry," she said. "We had to throw it out. The milk spoiled without a fridge."

"*Awww,*" wailed the friends together.

"What about soda?" Henry asked.

"We have some, but it's not cold," Mom replied.

Lukewarm soda? Yuck! Henry thought.

So Henry, Dudley, and Max had to settle on very boring glasses of water. They didn't even have ice cubes!

Back in the living room, Dudley pulled out his tablet. They played a rhythm-tapping game.

Henry tapped the blue notes. Max tapped the red ones. Dudley tapped the green *and* yellow notes, because he was a pro.

"Let's play again!" Max said after the first try.

Bloop! The screen suddenly went black.

"Oh no!" Dudley said. "My battery's dead. And we can't recharge it because there's still no power!"

Henry and Max folded their arms.

"Now what are we gonna do?" complained Henry. "We can't play video games or watch a movie."

The friends crawled into their sleeping bags. Henry pointed his flashlight at the ceiling. He held up his hand above the flashlight and lowered it.

"Eeeee!" Max and Dudley squealed as the giant shadow hand moved across the ceiling.

But even that got boring after a while.

Henry wiggled farther into his sleeping bag and sighed.

I wish my spell hadn't lasted THIS long, he thought.

Out loud, he said, "I guess there's nothing to do except sleep."

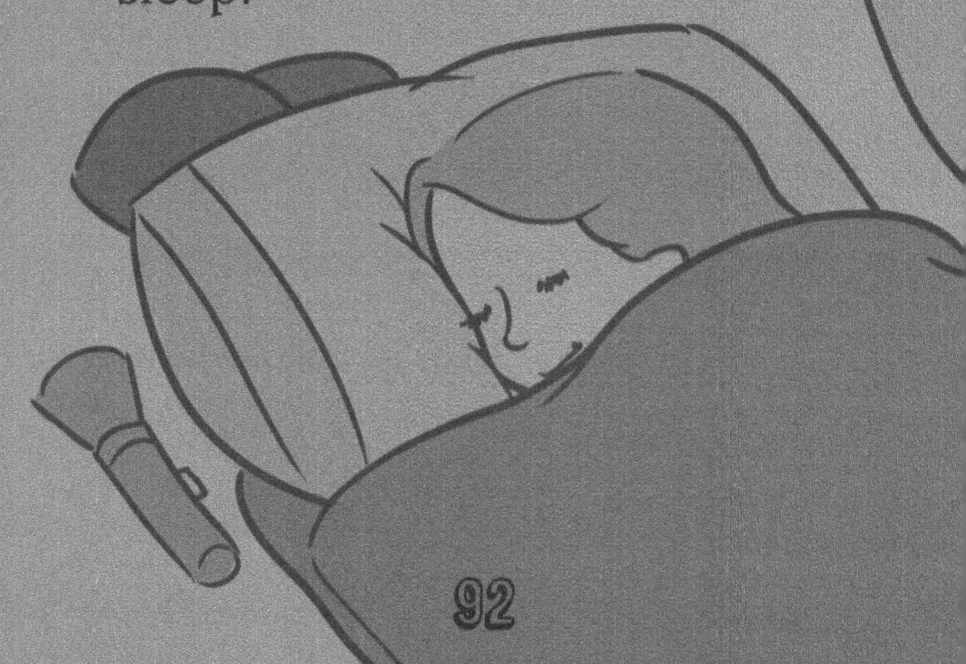

So Henry, Dudley, and Max said good night and switched off their flashlights.

Chapter 9

WHAT'S THAT NOISE?

The house was pitch-dark. There was no night-light, no hallway light, not even streetlight coming in from outside.

But there *were* noises.

Creak! Creak! Creak!

"What is that?" Dudley whispered.

The friends wriggled their sleeping bags closer together.

"It had better not be Heidi," Henry whispered back. "She pinky promised no more pranks!"

CREAK!

CREAK!

"Time for a spy mission!" Max said, unzipping her sleeping bag.

But Dudley grabbed Max's arm.

"What if it's a monster?"
Dudley whispered.

Henry gulped. Now he *really*
wished the power was back
on.

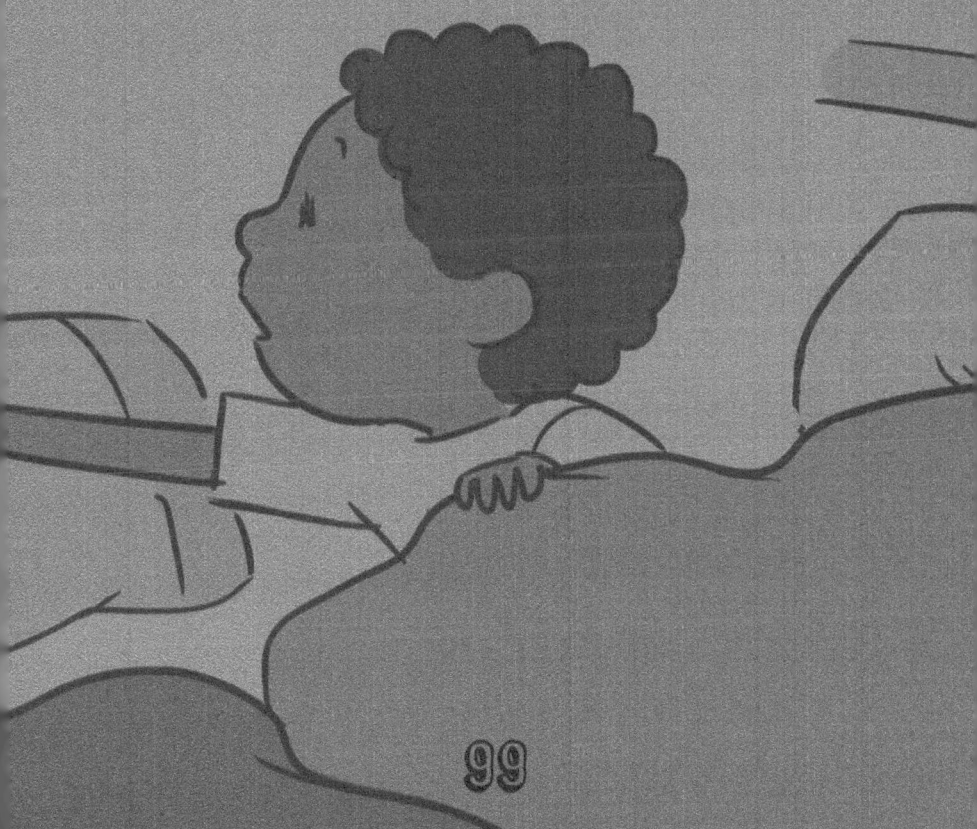

There was another noise—
only this one was HUGE.

CRAAAAAAASH! BLANG!

BAM! BONK! BONK!

"AAAAAAHHH!" They all
screamed.

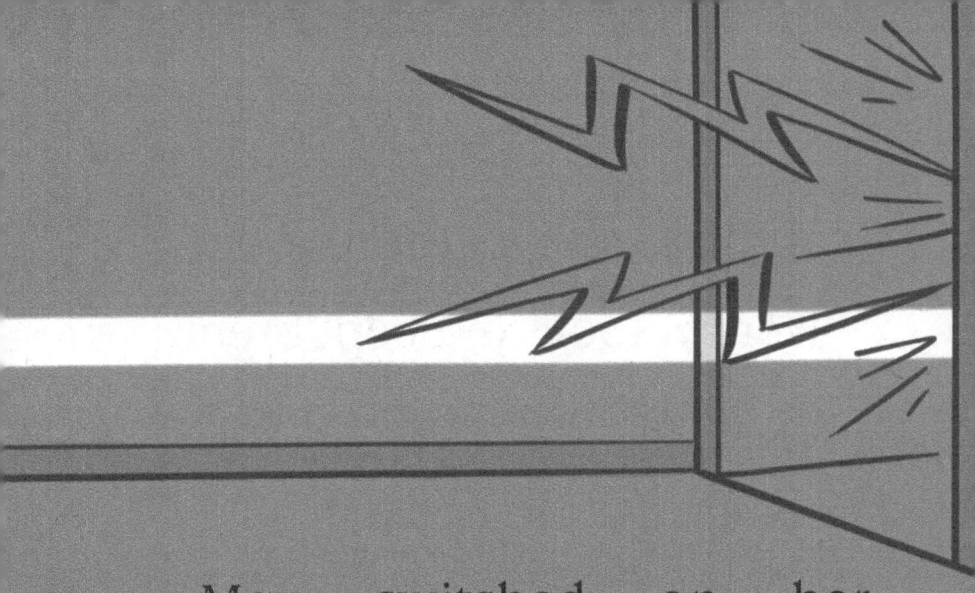

Max switched on her flashlight and started tiptoeing out of the room. The boys had no choice but to follow.

Henry swallowed hard as they made their way to the kitchen.

Something big and tall was standing next to the pantry.

Henry took a deep breath and yelled, "Get out, monster! This isn't your house!"

"But it IS my house!" the
monster yelled back.

Dudley shined the light on
the monster . . . revealing
Henry's dad!

A bunch of pasta boxes and cans lay on the floor at Dad's feet.

"I was looking for a snack," he explained. "But it's hard to see in the dark, and I knocked everything over."

"Busted!" said Henry, and everyone laughed.

"All right, back to bed with you all," Dad said. "I'll clean up this mess."

The three friends scampered back to the living room and jumped into their sleeping bags.

Henry closed his eyes again.
He could still hear little noises
coming from the kitchen.

But now that he knew it was
just his dad, he wasn't scared
anymore!

Chapter 10

RISE AND SHINE

Ding! Whirrrrrrrr! Hum-dum-dum-dum!

Henry's eyes popped open. The sun shined in from the living room window.

He knew those sounds.

It was the toaster, the blender, and Dad humming in the kitchen.

"Wake up!" Henry said to his friends. "The power is back on!"

Dudley yawned and sat up. "Aw, that means we have SCHOOL," Max said with a groan.

But Henry didn't care. He was excited to see everything back to normal.

The friends jumped out of their sleeping bags and went to the kitchen. Heidi was already sitting at the table eating breakfast.

"Hi, sleepyheads," she said.

Henry, Dudley, and Max were about to dig into their breakfasts when Mom cleared her throat.

"Aren't you all forgetting something to drink?" Mom asked, pulling out a carton from the fridge.

"It's STRAWBERRY MILK!"
Henry shouted, bouncing on
his chair.

"Fresh from the grocery store this morning," Mom said. She poured three glasses and set them on the table.

Henry raised his glass of strawberry milk.

"Cheers to the power coming back on!" he declared.

Henry and Dudley raised their glasses too. So did Heidi.

Clink! Clink! Clink! Clink!

"CHEERS!" they all shouted.

Check out the next book starring

HENRY HECKELBECK

"Look at all the boxes!" Henry Heckelbeck said to his best friend Dudley Day.

They were standing in Henry's garage, where a pile of cardboard boxes were stacked.

An excerpt from *Henry Heckelbeck Knights! Robots! Action!*

"You know what empty boxes mean!" Dudley said.

The two best friends locked eyes.

"BOX FORT!" they shouted.

The boys grabbed the boxes by the flaps. One by one, they dragged them into the living room.

"Let's build the world's biggest fort!" Henry said, stacking blankets from the hall closet into Dudley's waiting arms.

"Yeah!" Dudley agreed. "So big that Max won't even believe it!"

Max Maplethorpe, their other best friend, was coming over to play later.

The boys wanted to finish the fort before Max arrived.

An excerpt from *Henry Heckelbeck Knights! Robots! Action!*